SEVEN TALES
BY H. C. ANDERSEN

3982
And

Printed in the United States of America

Library of Congress Catalog Card Number: 59-16151

ISBN 0-06-023790-2
ISBN 0-06-023791-0 (lib. bdg.)
ISBN 0-06-443172-X (pbk.)

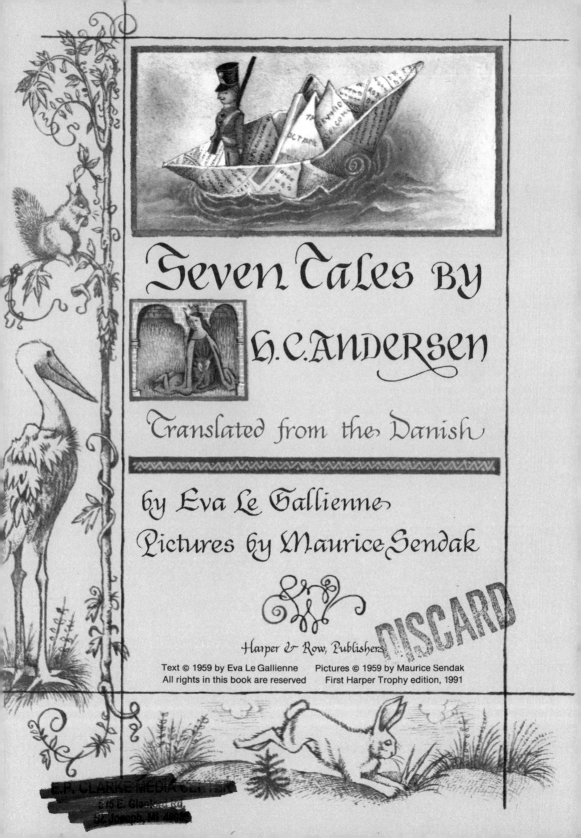

Seven Tales by H. C. Andersen

Translated from the Danish

by Eva Le Gallienne

Pictures by Maurice Sendak

Harper & Row, Publishers

FOREWORD

ONE DAY I was shopping in one of the large New York department stores when a little boy accompanied by his mother caught sight of me and stopping abruptly in the middle of the crowded aisle gave a shout of delighted recognition. "That's the lady whose mother sat on Hans Christian Andersen's knee!"

A few customers paused long enough to smile indulgently at the boy's mother—"What imagination these children have!" they seemed to say. But the little boy was right all the same. He had been present at the inauguration of the storytelling center in Central Park, where Hans Christian Andersen presides a good deal larger than life—in bronze—and had heard me tell the story. I never tired of hearing my mother tell it: the story of the time when, as a tiny little girl in her native Denmark, she had seen the old poet—a familiar yet already legendary figure—enter the classroom and

5

seat himself on the teacher's podium. He had surveyed the assembled children with his kind, tired eyes, and had picked out my mother as the smallest person there and beckoned her to come to him. He had helped her to climb onto his friendly, bony knee and had kept her there—now and then offering her a sip from the glass of barley water that stood on the table beside his chair—while for an enchanted hour he had told his fairy tales.

My mother never forgot this occasion—how could she!

Whenever she spoke of Hans Christian Andersen, there was a proprietary note in her voice; for this little girl of five had sensed the child in the old man. He had not seemed remote to her, or frightening, or strange; he was shy and simple just as she was.

Though he was a great man and famous throughout the world, his fame never ceased to fill him with a kind of puzzled wonderment, and his own life was to him the most miraculous of fairy tales.

Brief as it was, this meeting with Hans Christian Andersen, and the sense of comforting closeness that seems to have been a part of it, gave my mother, as she grew older, a feeling of having known the man; and this feeling she passed on to me.

I never think of Hans Christian Andersen as belonging to the past. If we allow ourselves really to look at a flower, a bird, a tree—as well as such creatures as snails, toads, moles and ants, to say nothing of such supposedly inanimate objects as darning needles, tops and balls, slates and slate pencils and, of course, tin soldiers—we will see Hans Christian Andersen alive in all of them.

To him everything had life and, because he listened, everything revealed its own particular story. He didn't make these stories up, he used to say— he only set down what was told him.

This faculty of sharing in the life of every creature and of every object is something that children understand. It is this faculty above all others that has made his stories so dear and familiar to them.

But his stories appeal to their elders too; for though Hans Christian Andersen had the rare quality of retaining a child's sense of wonder—the acute awareness of the myriad small miracles of which life is composed—the hardship and suffering of his early days, his Ugly-Duckling days, gave him a shrewd insight into the foibles of humanity: the petty cruelties, the vanities, the pretensions, the hypocrisies; and in many of his more humorous tales he revenged himself on his tormentors by drawing their portraits in the guise of wicked black imps, gossiping hens and bragging roosters, pompous old geese and belligerent turkey cocks. Children take these stories literally and enjoy them as such; we older folk often recognize in these satirical fables our relatives, our friends, and not infrequently, if we are honest enough to admit it, ourselves!

It is this double appeal that gives Hans Christian Andersen an audience ranging in age from eight to eighty; an audience that inhabits every part of the globe—for the stories of this Ugly Duckling who turned out to be a Swan have been translated into every known language. Why then, people may ask, should I have the temerity to add to the already numerous English versions? A hard question to answer!

Perhaps it is because I am an actor and have frequently told these stories from the stage; and, as an actor, I am acutely aware of the ring of words, the rhythms of speech. I have found most of the existing versions of these stories difficult to handle; they seem to me to have a foreign sound. This may be because the best known translations have been made by Danes, and the music of a Dane's English can never wholly succeed in being English music.

In Denmark Andersen is considered a great poet, as well as a great storyteller. His style is deceptively simple and, like most beautiful things, quite effortless; there is no trace of affected whimsicality. Danish is a cozy language, peculiarly fitted to convey the blend of poetry, common sense, and sly humor so typical of Hans Christian Andersen, as well as of the Danish people. Inevitably much of the flavor of his style is lost in translation, and I'm sure that those who have attempted to convey it have done so, as I do now, in deep humility.

Yet even though he must suffer a sea change in coming to us, we cannot do without him! He belongs not only to the children, but to all of us; not only to Denmark, but to the world.

E. Le Gallienne
Westport, Connecticut
April 1958

ARTIST'S FOREWORD

I HAVE OFTEN been asked, "How does one go about illustrating a children's book?" My answer is never more illuminating than, "Well, that depends on the book I'm illustrating." And it does, for aside from drawing with a pencil on a piece of drawing board, I have no simple answer, no formula that can be applied to all books. One can only consider the separate aspects.

The illustrator is essentially a collaborator. His first considerations are the story he is illustrating and the point of view of the writer. He must then go about creating pictures that are in harmony with this point of view; that give through color and imagery a further understanding of the story.

The art of illustration can be likened to any of the other interpretive arts, for example, singing. The vocal artist, too, is basically illuminating a story. Beauty of expression, vocal technic, and sympathetic understanding create a color and emotional depth which enlarge our understanding. So the illustrator creates, with technic and imagination, an added dimension to the child's pleasure and understanding. But how does one appeal to a child's understanding? Of the innumerable books for children that attempt just this, I would like, for the sake of clarity, to generalize and divide them into two groups under the headings "basic" and "dimensional." Perhaps these are not the best terms, but they do express the main points of difference.

The basic book deals in various and ingenious ways with the facts of the child's world. When illustrating a basic book, the artist must conscientiously stay within the limits of its purpose. Within that well-defined line he can enhance or destroy the total effect. He must create a harmonious balance between pictures and words to anticipate the exact moment at which the child will most want to "see what it looks like."

The dimensional book presents a much more enlarged picture of life. It is written on many different levels and demands more from the illustrator than a literal transcription of words into pictures. H. C. Andersen is a dimensional writer. With exquisite art he blends into perfect harmony two separate levels of the meaning of experience. On one he speaks directly to the child, presenting him with facts and fancies that stay close within the narrow boundaries of his experience. The adult can perceive that Andersen is simultaneously depicting a deeper moral and emotional experience. The child's inability to distinguish between phantasy and reality allows him to accept the story as literal truth. A fir tree is a fir tree. For the adult, the fir tree is equally the symbol Andersen uses to describe a tragic, human dilemma. These stories grow more meaningful as we grow more discerning.

Andersen's comments on life are mostly sad or gently ironical, rarely happy. This attitude colors but never distorts his vision. Writing for children did not mean diluting his personal vision but embodying it in concrete, literal terms so that we have a story, not an allegory. This was a matter of craft. His deceptively simple style, the terse, jaunty prose, the fresh and revealing manner (so like the child's) with which he viewed the world as though seen for the first time, his shrewd observance of detail —all were a matter of laborious writing. Andersen never believed that writing for children was any easier than writing for adults. In fact, I doubt he ever consciously wrote in a manner considered suitable for children. He simply wrote. There is no condescension here. There is morality, but it is not pretentious. There is sentiment, not sentimentality.

The Andersen illustrator must take all these factors into account. He can then allow himself the great satisfaction of acting as interpreter, with the one qualification that he never lose sight of the literal aspect of the stories. This very point represented my major problem. The stories offered such unlimited opportunities for dramatic interpretation that it was easy to overlook their more graphic qualities.

The fir tree, the tin soldier, and the ugly duckling represented symbols to be interpreted for their larger meanings. But my first pictures were all wrong. They seemed lifeless and thin, unequal to the job of supporting the stories. I had to go back to Andersen. The answer lay in the solid realism of his phantasy. I had underestimated the power of that realism. The duckling, despite its deeper significance, is a very substantial little bird. It must be acknowledged not merely as a symbol, but as a living creature. It became, then, a matter of combining both elements, the literal and the symbolic, of attempting in pictures what Andersen successfully achieves in words. I gave special attention to the note of sadness in Andersen and allowed it to determine my choice of colors. It seemed to me I could make use of detail much the same as Andersen did in order to solidify my own pictorial images.

These are some of the basic considerations that led up to the illustrating of this book. Thereafter the creative instinct took over and for that there are no definitions. I could never explain why I chose a medieval setting for my pictures. It just felt right, or so my instinct told me, and I can only hope it seems right to the reader.

Maurice Sendak
New York, N. Y.
November 1958

15

CONTENTS

The Fir Tree   19

The Princess and the Pea   47

Happy Family   51

The Ugly Duckling   63

The Darning Needle   93

It's Absolutely True!   105

The Steadfast Tin Soldier   114

THE FIR TREE

FAR OUT in the forest stood the most charming little fir tree. It had plenty of room to grow in, lots of sunshine, and all the fresh air it wanted, and it was sur-rounded on all sides by tall, sturdy com-rades, pine trees as well as firs. But this particular little fir tree was so anxious to grow up that it gave no thought to the warm sunshine or the fresh air; and it paid no attention to the merry chatter of the children who came into the woods looking for wild strawberries or blackberries. When they had gathered a whole bowlful, they often sat down by the little tree and threaded the berries on long straws, like rows of beads. "What a sweet little baby tree!" they cried. But the fir tree didn't like that, and refused to listen.

The following year it shot up a couple of feet and threw out a circle of new branches; and the year after, it added an even longer section to its stem, and threw out another circle of green. You can always tell the age of a fir tree by the number of sections it has between its branches.

"If only I were a great big tree like all those others!" sighed the little tree. "I'd

spread my branches far and wide, and my top would gaze out into the great world. Birds would build nests in my branches, and I would bow gracefully in the wind, as those other trees do!"

It took no delight in the sunshine, or the birds, or the rosy clouds that sailed over its head.

Sometimes in the winter when the ground sparkled with snow, a hare would come by and hop right over the little tree— how humiliating that was! But by its third winter it was already so tall that the hare was obliged to go round it. Oh! To grow up, to grow up, to grow big, to grow old— how wonderful that would be, the little tree thought!

In the fall the woodcutters came and felled some of the largest trees. This hap-

pened every year, and the young fir, who was by now quite tall, trembled with fear as the noble trees crashed to the ground. Their branches were lopped off and they looked quite thin and naked; you could scarcely recognize them. Then the men loaded them onto great wagons and the horses dragged them away out of the forest.

Where were they being taken? What was going to happen to them?

When spring came round again, and the stork and the swallows arrived, the little tree asked: "What happened to them? Did you meet them anywhere?"

The swallows knew nothing about it, but the stork looked thoughtful and nodded his head. "Yes, I think I know," he said. "I passed several new ships as I flew back from Egypt, and I noticed their tall splendid

22

masts. Those were probably the trees you speak of—there was a smell of pine about them. They looked very proud and stately, and sent you their greetings."

"If only I were big enough to sail across the sea! Tell me about the sea! What does it look like?"

"It's much too vast to describe," answered the stork, and he went on his way.

"Rejoice in your youth!" said the sunbeams. "Rejoice in your beauty and strength and in the young life that is in you!"

And the wind kissed the fir tree, and the dew shed tears over it—but the fir tree didn't understand.

Each year, just before Christmas, many of the very young trees were chopped down. Some of them were even younger and smaller than our fir tree, and it grew more and more restless—its one thought was to get away. It noticed that these young trees were chosen especially for their beauty, and they were allowed to keep their branches. The men loaded them carefully onto the wagons, and the horses dragged them away out of the forest.

"Where are they going?" asked the fir tree. "They're no bigger than I am—there was one of them that was even smaller. Why were they allowed to keep their branches? Where are they being taken to?"

"We know! We know!" chirruped the sparrows. "When we were in the city, we peeped in at the windows—we know where they're going! You can't imagine the splendor and glory that awaits them! We've peeped in at the windows and we've seen them! They'll be planted in the center of a

warm room and decked out with lovely decorations—with gilded apples, gingerbread, toys, and hundreds of bright candles!"

"And after that?" asked the fir tree, its branches quivering with excitement. "What happens after that?"

"We don't know what happens after that," answered the sparrows. "That was as much as we saw, but it was a gorgeous sight!"

"I wonder if I shall ever know such splendor!" cried the fir tree. "That sounds even more wonderful than sailing on the sea! Why can't it be Christmas now! I'm just as tall and handsome as those trees they took last year; why shouldn't *I* be loaded onto a wagon? Why shouldn't *I* be planted in a warm room and decked out with splendid

ornaments? And then—after that? Something even more wonderful must surely happen after that! They wouldn't take the trouble to decorate me unless something even more splendid was in store! But what? What? I long to know! I can't bear not to know!"

"Rejoice in us!" sang the fresh air and the sunshine. "Rejoice in your young strength and in your freedom!"

But the fir tree refused to rejoice. It grew taller and taller. Summer and winter it stood there green and beautiful—dark green and beautiful. Everyone who saw it cried out: "What a lovely tree!" and when Christmas came round again it was the first to be cut down. The ax cut deep into its very core, and it sank to the ground with a sigh. The pain made it feel faint, and it was quite unable to think of any happiness to come. It was overwhelmed with sorrow at the thought of leaving home—the spot where it had sprung to life. It knew now that it would never see any of its dear old comrades again, or the little bushes and the delicate flowers that grew around it. Perhaps it would never even see the birds again. The leave-taking was anything but pleasant.

When the fir tree came to itself again, it was lying in a yard with all the other trees. They had been unloaded from the wagon. It heard a man's voice cry out: "We'll take that one! That's a beauty!" Presently two servants in full livery came to fetch it, and carried it into a large, handsome drawing-room. There were oil paintings on the walls and the great porcelain stove was flanked

27

by huge Chinese vases with lions carved on their covers. There were rocking chairs, brocaded sofas, and several large tables littered with picture books, and toys worth hundreds of thousands of dollars—at least that's what the children said. The fir tree was placed in a big tub filled with sand, but you'd never have guessed it was a tub, for it was festooned with some green material and stood in the center of a gorgeous carpet. The tree was quivering with excitement. What was going to happen now? The young ladies of the house, assisted by the servants, began to trim it. They decked it with little baskets woven out of colored paper, and each basket was filled with candies. Gilded apples and walnuts hung from its boughs—you'd have thought they were actually growing there! Then over a hundred red and white and blue candles were fastened to its branches. There were dolls too—little dolls carved so realistically they might have been alive. The fir tree had never seen anything so dainty. And finally, at the very top of the tree, glistened a huge tinsel star! It was magnificent! Simply magnificent!

Everyone exclaimed: "Wait till this evening! This evening we'll light the candles—then everything will glitter!"

"If only it were evening now!" thought the tree. "If only it were time to light the candles! I wonder what happens after that? I wonder if any of the trees from the forest will come and admire me? Or if the sparrows will peep in at me through the windows? I wonder if I'm to remain here summer and winter decked out in all my glory?"

It kept on wondering so many things that its bark began to ache. And when a tree gets a bark-ache, it's just as painful as a headache is to us.

At last they lit the candles and the tree stood shimmering in a blaze of light. It was trembling so much with joy that a candle set fire to one of its twigs and gave it a good scorching.

The young ladies started to scream, and quickly put out the flame. The tree was careful not to tremble any more, though that wasn't easy, it was so overcome by its own radiance. But it was afraid it might shake off some of its ornaments, so it struggled to be calm. Suddenly the folding doors were opened wide and dozens of children burst into the room. They flung themselves at the tree with such a rush that they almost knocked it over. They were followed by the grownups, who fortunately had better manners. For a moment the children stood speechless with wonder, then they began to shout and sing. They danced round and round the tree snatching the presents off its boughs.

"What are they doing?" said the tree to itself. "What's going to happen now?" Gradually, as the candles burned down to the branches, they were put out one by one. Then came the signal to strip the tree, and the children attacked it with such violence that its branches creaked and groaned, and if it hadn't been fastened by a nail to the ceiling, it would certainly have toppled over.

The children went jumping about the room, admiring their lovely new toys, and no one seemed to notice the tree any more. The old nurse was the only one who paid any attention to it—she went snooping about among its boughs to see if by chance a fig or an apple had been forgotten there.

"A story! We want a story!" shouted the children as they surrounded a little fat man and pulled him towards the tree. He sat down beneath it. "Now we can pretend we're in the forest," he said, "and if the tree wants to, it can listen too! But I shall tell only one story. Which shall it be? Hey-Diddle-Diddle or Humpty-Dumpty and the Princess?"

"Hey-Diddle-Diddle!" cried some. "Humpty-Dumpty and the Princess!" cried others. And they shouted and laughed and screamed themselves hoarse. But the fir tree kept very still. "Am I not to share in the fun?" it thought. "Am I to have no part in it at all?" But it had already played its part, and had had its share of the fun.

Then the little fat man told about Humpty-Dumpty, and how he was kicked downstairs; and how, in spite of that, he married the princess and became a king. The children clapped their hands and shouted: "Another! We want another!" They wanted to hear Hey-Diddle-Diddle too. But the little fat man wouldn't tell any more, so they had to be satisfied with Humpty-Dumpty.

The fir tree stood thoughtful and silent. It had never heard the birds in the forest tell a story like that. "Humpty-Dumpty fell downstairs, and yet he succeeded in winning the princess. So that's how things happen in the world!" it said to itself. "The story must surely be true or that nice man would never have told it! Who knows? Perhaps *I* shall fall downstairs and win the hand of a princess!" And it looked forward to the next day. It was sure it would be decorated all over again, hung with lovely toys, tinsel, and gilded fruit, and lighted with hundreds of candles.

It made up its mind: "Tomorrow I shan't tremble! Tomorrow I shall rejoice in all my splendor! I'll hear the story of Humpty-Dumpty again, and perhaps the one about Hey-Diddle-Diddle too!" And all night long it remained quiet, deep in thought.

Early the next morning a footman came in, followed by a maid.

"They're going to decorate me again!" thought the tree. But instead, they hauled it out of the room and up to the attic. They stuck it in a dark corner where there wasn't even a ray of light. "I wonder what this means?" thought the tree. "What am I supposed to do here? What kind of excitement can there be in a place like this?" It leaned against the wall and went on thinking; and it had plenty of time to think, for days and nights went by and not a soul came near it. Once someone came up, but it was only to store away some big trunks in another part of the attic. The tree was left there hidden away, apparently forgotten.

"It's winter now," thought the tree. "The ground is hard and covered with snow. They couldn't possibly plant me now. I suppose that's why they're keeping me here until the spring. It's really very thoughtful of them. How kind people are! If only it weren't so dark here, and so dread-

35

fully lonely! There's not even a little hare to keep me company! It was nice out there in the forest when the snow lay on the ground and the little hares went hopping by. I shouldn't even mind their hopping over me—though I didn't like it at the time! If only it weren't so lonely here!"

"Peep, peep!" squeaked a little mouse as it crept cautiously out of its hole. It was joined by another little mouse. They sniffed at the base of the fir tree and then climbed about among its branches.

"It's very cold up here!" said the little mice. "Otherwise it's rather pleasant. Don't you think so too, old fir tree?"

"I'm not old," said the fir tree. "Heaps of trees are much older than I am!"

"Where do you come from?" asked the mice. "And what do you know?" They were frightfully inquisitive! "Tell us all about the most beautiful place in the world! Have you ever been there? Have you ever been in the larder where the shelves are full of cheeses, and where smoked hams hang from the rafters, and where you can dance on a floor made of wax candles? You go in there thin, and you come out fat!"

"No. I don't know any place like that," answered the fir tree. "But I know the forest where the sun shines and the birds sing!" And it told them about its childhood. The little mice listened attentively— they'd never heard anything like it. "What things you've seen!" they cried. "What happiness you've known!"

"I?" said the fir tree. And it went over in its mind what it had just been telling them. "Yes! Those were very pleasant days, now that I look back on them." But then it told them about Christmas Eve, and how it was decorated with cakes and candles.

"My goodness! How happy you must have been, old fir tree!" cried the little mice.

"I tell you I'm not old!" said the tree. "I just came out of the forest. I'm rather tall for my age, that's all!"

"You tell such lovely stories!" said the little mice, and the next night they came back with four other mice who wanted to hear about the tree's adventures. And the more it talked, the more clearly it remembered the past: "Yes! Those were pleasant days!" it said. "But there are even better times ahead! After all, though Humpty-Dumpty fell downstairs, he won the princess in the end! Perhaps I shall marry a

princess too!" And it remembered a charming little birch tree that grew near it in the forest. "Just like a lovely little princess!" it thought.

"Who is Humpty-Dumpty?" asked the little mice. Then the fir tree told them the whole story—it remembered every single word of it. The little mice were so pleased that they climbed to the very top of the tree and danced about with delight. The following night a lot more mice came, and on Sunday two rats joined the party. But they found the Humpty-Dumpty story dull, and this so upset the little mice that they began to have doubts about it too.

"Is that the only story you know?" asked the rats.

"Yes, that's the only one," answered the tree. "I heard it on the happiest evening of my life, but I didn't realize then how happy I was."

"It's a terribly dull story! Don't you know any about bacon? Or tallow candles? No larder stories?"

"I'm afraid not," said the tree.

"Let's go!" said the rats, and they went back to their homes.

The little mice stopped coming too, and the tree said to itself with a sigh: "It was nice when the little mice were here—gathered all round me, listening to me talk! Now that's over too! When I get back into the world again—out of this place—I must remember always to enjoy things!"

But when would that be? At last, one morning, some people came to clear out the attic. They moved a lot of trunks and boxes, and the tree was pulled out of its corner.

They didn't treat it very nicely. It was thrown roughly to the floor and dragged towards the stairs, but at least it saw daylight.

"Now life is beginning again!" thought the tree. It felt the fresh air and for the first time in many months the sunbeams played on it. It was taken out to the courtyard. This all happened so quickly that the tree quite forgot to look at itself—there was so much to see out there. The yard gave onto a garden in full bloom. The roses hung in fragrant clusters along the little fence, the lime trees were in bloom, and the swallows flew overhead twittering: "Kree-ree! Kree-ree! Here comes my love!" But they weren't referring to the fir tree.

"Now I can begin to live!" exclaimed the fir tree, rejoicing, and it stretched out its branches. Alas, they were all brown and withered! It was lying in a corner of the yard on a bed of nettles. The tinsel star was still fastened to its topmost branch and glittered in the bright sunshine.

Some children were playing in the court-yard—those same happy children who had danced round the tree on Christmas Eve and had taken such delight in it. The littlest one made a dash for the tinsel star and tore it off.

"Look what I found on the ugly old Christmas tree!" he cried, and he jumped up and down on the withered branches.

The tree looked at the radiant flowers blooming in the garden, then it looked at itself and wished it were back in its dark corner in the attic. It thought of its own radiant youth in the forest, of the glorious

43

Christmas Eve, and of the little mice that had listened so eagerly to the story of Humpty-Dumpty.

"Over! All over!" cried the poor tree. "How foolish I was not to appreciate my happiness! Now it's over! All over!"

The gardener's boy came and chopped the tree up into small pieces. It made quite a large stack of wood. He built a fire with it under the big kettle—it made a splendid blaze! As it burned the tree heaved deep sighs, and each sigh sounded like a faint shot. The children ran in, attracted by the sound, sat round the fire and gazed into it shouting: "Piff, paff!" And with each explosion, which was really a sigh, the tree remembered a lovely summer day in the forest, or a night in winter under the stars. It thought of Christmas Eve and the story of Humpty-Dumpty—the only story it had ever heard, the only story it had ever told. Then the tree was burned to ashes.

The children went back to the yard to play, and the littlest one wore on his breast the tinsel star, the same star the tree had worn on the happiest evening of its life. So that was the end of the tree, for sooner or later all things come to an end—including our story.

THE PRINCESS
AND THE PEA

ONCE UPON A TIME there was a prince who wanted to find himself a princess. But, of course, she would have to be a real, genuine princess. So he went all over the world in search of one.

Goodness knows, there were plenty of princesses, but it was hard to tell whether they were the real thing or not. Each time

47

he thought he'd found one, she would say or do something that made him suspect she might be a phony. At last he went back home again. He was very disappointed and discouraged, for he did so want to find himself a princess—that is, a real genuine one.

One night there was a dreadful storm. The thunder roared, the lightning flashed, and the rain came down in buckets. It was quite terrifying. Then, suddenly, there was a knock at the great gate of the town, and the old king himself went down to open it. And there, outside the gate, stood a princess. But, my goodness, what a sight she was! Her clothes were soaked right through, her hair was dripping wet, and the water poured in at the toes of her shoes and out at the heels. And yet she kept repeating that she was a princess.

48

"We'll soon find out about that!" said the old queen. She didn't say a word to anyone, but went straight in to the guest room; there she took all the bedclothes off the bed and carefully placed a tiny pea under the mattress. She piled twenty mattresses on top of it, and on top of the twenty mattresses she piled twenty down comforters, and then she went back and told the princess that her bed was ready.

The next morning she asked the princess how she had slept. "Slept!" cried the princess. "I didn't sleep a wink! I couldn't close my eyes all night—heaven knows what was in that bed! I feel as though I'd been lying on a rock—I'm black and blue from head to foot. It's awful!"

That was certainly proof enough. They all knew then that she must be a real prin-

49

cess. Otherwise she could never have felt that tiny pea through twenty mattresses and twenty down comforters. Only a real, genuine princess could be that sensitive.

So the prince took her for his wife and they lived happily ever after.

The pea was placed in a glass case in the art museum. It's probably still there—that is, unless someone has stolen it.

How's that for a story?

HAPPY FAMILY

IN THIS COUNTRY, of all the leaves, the dock leaf is certainly the largest. Hold it in front of your little tummy and it's as good as an apron. Hold it over your head when it's raining, and it's almost as good as an umbrella. That's how big a dock leaf is! And a dock leaf never grows alone. Where there is one there are bound to be others— they're a beautiful sight—and all that

51

beauty is food for snails. Those large white snails that distinguished people in the old days made into tasty fricassées and devoured with cries of "Oh, how delicious!" lived exclusively on dock leaves. And that's why the dock leaves were planted.

Now there was once an old manor house where snails were no longer eaten—they had died out. But the dock leaves hadn't died out. They grew and they spread. They overran all the paths and all the flower beds. There was no controlling them! The place became a regular dock leaf forest. If it hadn't been for an occasional apple or plum tree, no one would have dreamed there had ever been a garden there. As far as the eye could see spread the dock leaf forest, and in the very center of this forest lived two very old snails—the last of their line.

52

They were so old that they had forgotten just how old they were, but they remembered they had once been part of a large family that had come from a foreign land, and it was for them that the dock leaves had originally been planted. They had never been outside the forest, but they knew that somewhere in the world there was something called the Manor House. This was a place where one was cooked, became quite black, and was served on a silver dish—but no one had ever found out what happened after that. They couldn't quite imagine what it would be like to be cooked and served on a silver dish, but it was thought to be a delightful experience and, above all, most distinguished. The cockroaches, toads, and earthworms they had consulted in the matter could give them no informa-

53

tion. None of them had ever been cooked —much less served on a silver dish.

The two old white snails realized that they were the most distinguished creatures in the world. How could it be otherwise when the whole dock leaf forest had been planted just for them and the Manor House existed simply that they might be cooked and served on silver dishes?

They lived in solitary splendor and were very happy, and since they had no children of their own, they adopted an ordinary little snail and brought him up as their own son. But he never seemed to grow any larger— probably because he was too common. The old Mother Snail, however, fancied she noticed a slight increase in his size, and asked Father Snail—who couldn't seem to notice any difference—to measure the little snail's shell. So he measured it and found that, as usual, Mother Snail was right.

One day it was pouring rain.

"Just listen to it drum-rum-rumming on the dock leaves!" said old Father Snail.

"The dock leaves are leaking!" said Mother Snail. "The water is running down the stalks. It'll be quite wet down here! How lucky we are to have our own good houses—and the little one has his own house too. We have much to be grateful for; we are the most privileged of creatures! It's obvious that we are nature's aristocrats! We are born with a house on our back, and this wonderful dock leaf forest was planted especially for us! I wish I knew just how large it is, and what lies beyond it."

"There's nothing beyond it," said Father Snail. "No place on earth could possibly compare with this. It satisfies me completely—I have no desire to know of any other."

"All the same," said Mother Snail, "I shouldn't mind going to the Manor House and being cooked and served on a silver dish. All our ancestors were honored so—it must be a very remarkable experience."

"I expect the Manor House has crumbled into ruins," said Father Snail. "Either that or the dock leaves have swallowed it up, together with its inhabitants. You're so strenuous—you're always in such a hurry! And the little one's caught the habit too. For three whole days he's been climbing up that stalk! It gives me a headache just to watch him!"

"Don't be such a scold!" said Mother Snail. "Look how sedate he is—how dignified! After all, he's the only child we have! We'll live to be very proud of him—you'll see! But that reminds me: what shall we do about finding him a wife? Surely we must have some relatives left somewhere in the forest."

"There are plenty of black snails, of course," answered Father Snail. "Black snails without houses—vulgar creatures! But they're stuck-up all the same! We might speak to the ants about it; they're always running back and forth pretending to be busy. Perhaps they could find a suitable wife for our little one."

"We know of a most enchanting creature," said the ants. "But it wouldn't work out. You see, she happens to be a queen!"

"That makes no difference," said the old snails. "But are you sure she has a house?"

"She has a palace," answered the ants, "the most beautiful ant-palace, with seven hundred separate entrances!"

"You don't expect our son to live in an anthill!" said Mother Snail. "If that's all you have to suggest, we'll consult the gray gnats. Rain or shine, they're always on the wing. They fly all over the forest and are familiar with every part of it."

"Yes, indeed! We know a wife for him!" said the gnats. "A hundred paces from here —man's paces, that is—a charming little snail, complete with her own house, is sitting on a gooseberry bush. She's alone in the world and is just the right age to think of marriage. It's only a hundred paces from here, that's all!"

"She must come to him," said the old

snail. "After all, he owns a dock leaf forest; all she has is a bush!"

So the gnats went to fetch the little snail-maiden. It took her eight whole days to make the journey; but this delighted the old snail—such deliberation was a sign of breeding.

So they celebrated the wedding. Six glow-worms did their best to give a festive light, but apart from this it was a very quiet affair. The old snails would tolerate no frivolity. Mother Snail made a most edifying speech, but Father Snail couldn't say a word—he was too deeply moved. As a wedding gift the young couple were given the whole dock leaf forest, and the old snails repeatedly assured them that it was the loveliest place on earth. They advised them to live a respectable and worthy life—and, above all, to multiply. Then, someday, they and their children might hope to reach the Manor House—there to be cooked till they were black, and served on silver dishes.

Having delivered these instructions, the old snails retired into their respective houses and went to sleep. They never came out again.

The young snails reigned over the dock leaf forest, and had innumerable children —but none of them was ever cooked or served on a silver dish. So they came to the conclusion that the Manor House must have fallen into ruins, and that all of mankind had died out. And since no one contradicted them, this was obviously true. The rain beat down on the dock leaves and drummed out music just for them; and the sun shone on the dock leaves and made them glow with bright colors just for them, and they were very happy. Yes! The whole family was very, very happy!

THE UGLY DUCKLING

I T WAS LOVELY in the country; it was summertime. The wheat was golden, the oats were green, the hay was stacked in the green meadows, where the stork clambered about on his long red legs jabbering away in Egyptian—for that was the language his mother taught him. The meadows were surrounded by great forests, and deep within

the forests were many lakes. Yes, it was certainly lovely in the country!

An old manor house stood bathed in sunshine. It was encircled by deep moats filled with water, and from the water's edge to the foot of the walls the banks were covered with huge dock leaves. Some of them were so tall that little children could easily stand upright beneath them. They formed a dense wilderness—a regular forest—and in the center of that wilderness, well hidden away, a duck was sitting on her nest. She was busy hatching her eggs. She'd been there a long time and she was beginning to get sick of it. She'd had very few visitors, for most of the other ducks had such fun swimming about in the moats they couldn't be bothered to sit under the dock leaves gossiping with her.

At last the eggshells began to crack, one after the other; and suddenly all the egg yolks had turned into little ducks. They stuck out their heads and cried: "Peep! Peep!"

"Quack, quack! Quick, quick!" the mother duck answered. And the baby ducks struggled out of the shells as fast as they could and stared in wonder at the green leaves. Green is so good for the eyes that their mother let them stare as much as they liked.

"My! How big the world is!" the ducklings cried. And they certainly had more room now than when they were cooped up in their eggshells.

"There's more to the world than this!" said their mother. "The world stretches all the way across the garden and even beyond it, right into the big field by the parsonage. I've never been that far myself, though! Well? Are you all here?" she continued, and she stood up to take a look. "No! I'm not through yet! That big egg over there is still unhatched. How much longer will it take? I declare I'm getting sick of it!" And she plunked herself down again.

"How are we getting on?" asked an elderly duck who'd come to pay a call.

"There's one egg that's taking such a time!" said the duck on the nest. "It simply will not hatch! But just look at the others! Quite the loveliest ducklings I've ever seen —exactly like their father! The wretch! He never thinks of paying me a visit!"

"Let's have a look at that egg," said the old duck. "It'll turn out to be a turkey egg, you'll see! I was fooled like that once, and what I went through! Do you know that those creatures won't go near the water? They're actually afraid of it! I simply couldn't get them to go in. I quacked at them and I squawked at them—but it was no use! Let's have a look at it! Yes! That's undoubtedly a turkey egg! Don't bother with it! Take my advice and let it be!"

"I've sat on it this long, I suppose I might as well sit a little longer," said the duck with an impatient sigh.

"Have it your own way!" quacked the old duck, and she waddled off.

At last the big egg opened with a crack, and the baby tumbled out. "Peep! Peep!" he cried. He was very big and very ugly. The mother duck looked at him critically. "What an enormous duckling!" she said. "He's quite different from the others. I

wonder if he really is a turkey chick! Well, we'll soon find out! Into the water he'll go if I have to kick him in myself!"

Next day the weather was mild and lovely. The sun shone brightly on the green dock leaves. The mother duck appeared at the edge of the moat proudly leading her brood. Splash! And she was in the water. "Quack, quack! Quick, quick!" she cried, and one by one the little ones plunged in. The water closed over their heads, but only for a moment. Up they popped again and floated beautifully, using their legs like experts. They were all in the water now; even the ugly gray one was swimming too.

"Well! He's certainly no turkey chick!" thought the duck. "How nicely he uses his legs! And how well he carries himself—he's my child all right! And he's really quite handsome, once you get used to him! Quack, quack! Quick, quick! Now—follow me! I'm going to show you the world and introduce you to the duck yard; but stay close to me, or you might get stepped on; and watch out for the cat!"

Then she led them into the duck yard. The noise was deafening: two duck families were fighting over an eel head. But in the end the cat got it.

"That's life for you!" said the mother

duck, licking her beak. She wouldn't have minded a bit of eel herself.

"Use your legs!" she cried. "Come along now—keep moving! And be sure and arch your necks politely to that duck over there —she's a most important person. She comes of an old Spanish family—that's why she's so plump, you see. Notice the red band round her leg—a very great distinction! It's the highest honor a duck can aspire to; it means that her owner will never part with her, and that she is to be respected by man and beast! Keep moving! Turn out your toes! A well-bred duckling always walks with his toes well turned out—just as father and mother do! Now then! Bow your necks and say 'Quack!' "

They obeyed their mother's orders. But all the other ducks stared at them and ex-

claimed out loud: "Good Lord! Do we have to make room for them? As if it weren't crowded enough in here already! And what about that big one! Isn't he a sight! We can't be expected to put up with him!" And one of the ducks flew up and bit him in the neck.

"Leave him alone!" quacked the mother duck. "He's doing no harm!"

"He's much too big—he's a regular freak!" said the duck who'd done the biting. "We'll show him a thing or two!"

"Congratulations, mother!" said the old duck with the red band round her leg. "Your children are lovely! All but that last one. He didn't turn out too well. Can't you do something about him?"

"I'm afraid not, Your Grace," answered the mother duck. "He may not be handsome, but he has a wonderful nature; and he swims quite as well as any of the others —a little better, in fact. As he gets older his looks will improve, and he may even get a little smaller. He stayed in his egg too long, you see. I expect that affected his figure." She gave him a gentle little peck on the neck and straightened out his feathers. "And besides, he's a drake," she added, "and a drake's looks aren't so important. He's strong—that's the main thing! I feel sure he'll manage to make his way in the world!"

"Your other ducklings are charming," the old duck said. "Now, make yourselves at home! And if you should happen to find an eel's head, you may bring it to me!"

So they all made themselves at home.

But the poor duckling who was the last to come out of his egg, and who was so very

ugly, was bitten and badgered and made fun of—not only by the ducks but by the hens too. They all shouted at him: "He's too big! He's too big! He's much too big!" And the turkey cock who was born with spurs on, and fancied himself an emperor, blew himself up and bore down on him like a ship in full sail, scolding and gobbling away till his face grew purple with rage. The poor duckling didn't know what to do or where to go. He was miserably unhappy because he was so ugly and because they all made fun of him.

The first day was bad enough, but each day it grew worse. The poor duckling was chased from one end of the yard to the other. His brothers and sisters were mean to him too. "Hope the cat gets you—you ugly freak!" they shouted. And even his

73

mother said she wished she could get rid of him! The ducks bit him and the hens pecked him, and when the kitchen maid brought them their food, she kicked at him with her foot.

At last he could bear it no longer. He ran to the fence and managed to fly over it. When he landed in the bushes on the other side, all the little wild birds rose up in alarm. "It's because I'm so ugly!" thought the duckling, and he closed his eyes. But he kept on running all the same. At last he came to the big marsh where the wild ducks lived. He lay there all night, exhausted and miserable.

At dawn the wild ducks flew up to have a look at the stranger. They stood all round him and stared at him. "What kind of a duck do you think you are?" they asked. The duckling bowed politely to all sides. "You're certainly ugly enough!" the wild ducks cried. "But that's all right with us, as long as you don't try to marry one of our young ladies!" As if he had any thought of marrying, poor thing! All he asked was to be allowed to lie there in the reeds and drink a little marsh water.

He lay there two whole days, then two wild geese came along—or rather, wild ganders, for they were males. They hadn't been out of the egg very long and were feeling very cocky.

"Hey!" they cried. "You're so ugly we kind of like you! Don't you want to come with us and see a bit of life? There's another marsh near here full of pretty little geese.

They're all cute young things anxious to say 'Quack!' They might take to you—you're so ugly and so different!"

Bang! Bang! Two shots rang out, and both wild geese fell down in the reeds stone dead. The marsh water was stained with their blood. Bang! Bang! Two more shots! Whole flocks of wild geese rose up from the rushes. Bang! Bang! The shooting went on and on. The hunters lay in ambush all around the marsh. Some of them had even climbed up into the trees and were hidden in the branches that stretched far out over the reeds. The smoke rose in blue clouds against the dark trees and hung low over the water; the hound dogs came splashing through the mud, crushing down the reeds and the rushes. The poor duckling had never been so scared—he tried to hide his head under his wing. Suddenly a huge dog came right up to him. Its red tongue was lolling out of its mouth and its eyes were bright and fierce. Its great jaws with their gleaming white teeth seemed just about to close on him, then—with a splash—it went off and left him unharmed.

"Thank goodness!" sighed the duckling. "I'm so ugly even the dog would have none of me!"

And he lay there quite still while the shots rattled through the reeds as gun after gun was fired.

At last, quite late in the day, the shooting stopped. But the duckling was still afraid to move. It was several hours before he dared to look about him, and then he hurried away from the marsh as fast as he could go.

He ran over fields and through meadows, battling his way against the wind.

By evening he reached a small tumble-down farmhouse. It was so very old that it was actually falling apart. It was only because it couldn't make up its mind which way to fall that it remained standing. The wind had turned into a regular gale, and the duckling had to sit on his tail to keep from being blown away. And it was getting worse and worse. Suddenly he noticed that one of the hinges on the door had broken loose, and it wasn't tightly closed. There was a small crack on one side just large enough for him to squeeze through—and that's just what he did.

The little house belonged to a very old woman. She lived there with her cat and her hen. She called the cat "Sonnie." He could

arch his back and purr, and if you rubbed his fur the wrong way, he could even give out sparks. The hen had little squatty legs and was known as "Chicky-squat-legs." She laid fine eggs and the old woman loved her as if she'd been an only child.

Early the next morning the duckling was discovered, and the cat began to purr and the hen began to cluck.

"What's up? What's up?" asked the old woman peering round the room. She was half blind and she took the duckling for a nice fat duck that had gone astray. "What a bit of luck!" she said. "Now we'll have some duck eggs! Let's hope it's not a drake! Well, we'll soon find out!"

So she let the duckling stay on approval for three weeks—but no eggs came. The cat was the master of the house and the hen was the mistress. "We—and the world!" they used to say. They firmly believed that they were at least half the world—and by far the better half. The duckling had his own opinion on that score, but you couldn't contradict the hen—she wouldn't stand for that.

"Can you lay eggs?" she asked.

"No."

"Then you'd better hold your tongue!"

And the cat asked: "Can you arch your back, purr, and give out sparks?"

"No."

"Then you've no right to an opinion; leave that to your betters!"

So the duckling sat in a corner and felt very depressed. He got to thinking about the fresh air and the sunshine, and he was suddenly filled with such a longing to go swimming that he couldn't resist telling the hen about it.

"What's the matter with you?" she cried. "It's because you sit there doing nothing that you get these crazy notions! Just lay an egg or two—or learn to purr—then you'll be all right!"

"But it's such a wonderful feeling to glide over the water—to feel it close over your head as you dive to the bottom!"

"Have you lost your wits?" squawked the hen. "Swimming and diving, indeed! Just ask the cat, who's the cleverest person I know, what he thinks about swimming and diving! I'd hate to tell you what I think! Or ask the mistress—the old woman there—no one in the world is as clever as she is! Just ask her if she likes swimming and getting her head wet!"

"You don't understand me," said the duckling.

"Well, if we don't understand you, who

can, I'd like to know! Don't tell me you're any cleverer than the cat and the old woman —I say nothing of myself! You shouldn't be so stuck-up, child! You should thank your lucky stars that we've all been so kind to you! Here you are in this nice warm room in the company of people capable of teaching you a great deal, I'd have you know! And there you sit talking nonsense! If I tell you unpleasant truths, it's for your own good; unpleasant truths are a sure sign of friendship! So just you settle down and lay a few eggs; or learn to purr and give out sparks!''

"I think I'd rather go out into the world," said the duckling.

"Suit yourself!" said the hen.

So the duckling went on his way. He glided over the water and he dived into the cool depths. But wherever he went he was looked down on, because he was so ugly.

Fall came. The leaves in the woods turned yellow and brown; they were blown off the trees and they whirled and danced in the wind. The sky looked bleak; the clouds hung low, heavy with hail and snow. The ravens perched on the fences screaming "Av! Av!" with the cold. You got chilled to the bone if you let yourself think about it. The poor duckling had a hard time.

One evening, just as the sun was setting in all its glory, a whole flock of beautiful, majestic birds came out of the bushes. The duckling had never seen such lovely birds. They were dazzling white, with long graceful necks—they were swans. One of them gave an eerie cry, then they opened their great splendid wings and soared away, leaving the cold north far behind, flying towards sunny lands, with open lakes. They rose up into the air so high, so high! And as the ugly little duckling watched them a queer feeling came over him. He turned somersaults in the water, craned his neck trying to follow their flight, and uttered a cry so loud and strange that it quite frightened him. He was as though haunted by those beautiful birds—those happy birds. When he finally lost sight of them, he dived right down to the very bottom of the water; and when he came up again, he was quite beside himself. He had no idea what the birds were called or where they were going, he only knew that he loved them as he had never loved anything before. He was not envious of them—such beauty was not for him, poor ugly little thing! He'd have been only too grateful to have gone on living with the ducks, if they'd have been willing to put up with him.

The winter was cold—bitterly cold! The duckling swam around all day trying to keep the water from freezing over; but each night his swimming hole grew smaller and smaller. It was such a hard frost that everything seemed to snap and crackle. He kept on paddling frantically, but at last he became so exhausted that he lay quite still—and one night he was trapped in the ice.

Early the next morning a farmer happened to pass by. He saw the duckling, smashed the ice with his wooden shoe, rescued him, and took him home to his wife. There the poor duckling revived.

85

The farmer's children wanted to play with him, but the duckling was frightened and thought they meant to hurt him. He fled from them in terror and blundered right into the milk pail, splashing the milk all over the room. The farmer's wife screamed and waved her arms, so he flew into the butter tub and from there into the flour barrel. You can imagine what a sight

he was! The woman screamed again and went after him with the poker, and the children tumbled all over each other trying to catch him, laughing and shouting with delight. It was a good thing that the door had been left open—he darted out and hid himself in the bushes. He lay there on the snow for a while, in a daze.

To describe all the misery and hardship

the poor duckling went through that bitter winter would be too long and sad a tale. He had gone back to the marsh, and was lying among the reeds and rushes, when he felt the sun grow warm again and he heard the larks begin to sing. Spring had come at last.

Then quite suddenly he spread his wings. Never had they made that whirring sound, or borne him up so powerfully. Almost before he knew it, he found himself in a big garden. The apple trees were in full bloom and the air was filled with the scent of lilacs; their branches stretched out over a winding stream. Everything was beautiful in the fresh young green of spring! Then—quite close to him—out of a thicket came three lovely swans. They preened their feathers and floated gracefully over the water. As he recognized the beautiful birds a great sadness overwhelmed him.

"What noble birds!" he thought. "I'll fly over and join them. I'm so ugly I expect they'll tear me to pieces for daring to come near them. But I'd sooner be killed by them than be bitten by the ducks, pecked at by the hens, kicked by the kitchen maid, and suffer through another winter!" So he alighted on the water and swam towards the beautiful birds. When they saw him, they came sailing down on him with wings half-spread. "Kill me! I'm ready!" cried the poor duckling, and he bowed his head towards the stream, waiting for death. Then he saw his own reflection in the clear, sparkling water. And he saw that he was no longer awkward and drab and ugly. He saw that he, too, was a swan!

It isn't being born in a duck yard that matters: if you came out of a swan's egg, you'll be a swan just the same!

The duckling felt quite grateful for all the misery and suffering he'd been through. It made him better able to appreciate his present happiness and all the beauty that surrounded him. The great swans swam round him and stroked him with their beaks.

Some little children came down to the edge of the stream and threw pieces of bread to the birds. A little boy cried out: "Look! There's a new one!" And the others joined in. "A new one! A new one!" they shouted. They clapped their hands and danced about with joy; then they ran off to fetch their parents. When they came back, they all threw bread and cake into the water, and everyone exclaimed: "Look at the new one! He's so young and handsome—he's the loveliest one of all!"

He felt quite shy, and hid his head

under his wing. He was overwhelmed by so much happiness. But he wasn't a bit proud, for the pure in heart are without pride. It seemed strange, after having been ridiculed and tormented, to hear himself called the loveliest bird of all. The lilacs dipped their branches into the water as he passed. The blessed sun shone warm and bright. He preened his glistening white feathers, and his heart was full of joy as he murmured to himself: "No one would ever have dreamed that the Ugly Duckling could possibly turn out to be so happy!"

THE DARNING
NEEDLE

ONCE UPON A TIME there was a darning needle who was so full of airs and graces that she actually believed herself to be the finest kind of sewing needle.

"See that you handle me with care!" she said to the fingers as they took her out of the sewing basket. "If you should ever drop me, you'd never find me again—I'm so fine, I'm practically invisible!"

"That's what you think!" said the fingers as they grabbed her round the middle.

"Make way! Here I come followed by my suite!" said the darning needle, and she proudly drew the long thread after her. There was no knot on the end of it, but she refused to think about that.

The fingers steered the darning needle towards the cook's slipper. The leather was torn and needed mending.

"What vile work!" exclaimed the darning needle. "I'll never get through this leather. I shall break! I shall break! I know I shall break!" And break she did.

"What did I tell you?" cried the darning needle. "I said I was too delicate!"

"That's the end of her!" thought the fingers. But they were obliged to keep hold of her all the same while the cook put a bit of sealing wax on her broken end and stuck her in the front of her dress.

"Well! Now I've become a brooch!" said the darning needle. "I always knew I was destined for greatness. True worth always triumphs!" And she chuckled inwardly. Outwardly she remained unchanged—it's almost impossible to see a darning needle chuckle. She sat proudly on the cook's bosom, glancing loftily from side to side, as though she were riding in a carriage.

"Allow me to inquire—are you made of gold?" she asked of a pin who was her neighbor. "You're very handsome, and you've a head of your own; rather a small head, it's true—but perhaps in time it may grow larger. I realize we can't all be crowned with sealing wax!" As she said this, she was so filled with her own importance and drew herself up so proudly, that she fell headlong into the kitchen sink just as the cook was rinsing it out, and was swept down the drain and out into the gutter.

"We're off on a journey, I see!" she cried. "I only hope I shan't get lost." But lost she was.

"I've always known I was too delicate for this world," she said as she sat in the gutter. "Well—at least I know who I am! That's always a comfort." And the darning needle held herself very erect, and wasn't in the least downhearted.

All sorts of things drifted over her— sticks, bits of straw, and pieces of old news- paper. "Just look at them sailing by!" she said. "Little do they know what lies beneath them; little do they know that I am here! Take that stick, for instance. It has only one

thought in its head: 'stick'! It can think of nothing but itself. And look at that bit of straw whirling and twirling about! Don't be so pleased with yourself, my friend—you may find yourself crushed against the curbstone. And what about that old newspaper! Every word in it was forgotten long ago, and yet it spreads itself out as if it were the latest edition! Such self-importance! Yet here I sit quietly and patiently. I know who I am— I shall go on being myself forever!"

One day the darning needle noticed something glittering beside her in the gutter—she was certain it must be a diamond. Actually it was a bit of broken bottle; but because it glittered so splendidly she condescended to talk to it, and she introduced herself as a brooch.

"You must be a diamond," she said

amiably. "Yes—something of the sort," it replied. So they thought of each other as objects of the greatest value. They started to converse, and exchanged views on the haughtiness and arrogance of humanity.

"I once lived in a basket in the home of a certain gentlewoman," said the darning needle. "This gentlewoman was a cook. She had five fingers on each hand, and the conceit of those fingers was positively incredible! Yet their only purpose in life was to look after me—to lift me out of the basket, and place me back in it again."

"Tell me—did they glitter?" asked the bit of glass.

"Glitter! I should think not!" answered the darning needle. "But the arrogance of them! They were five brothers—their family name was 'Finger.' They stood stiffly side by side, but they were all of different lengths. One of them was called 'Thumb'—he was short and fat, and was out of line with the others. He had only one joint in his back and could only bow from the waist, and yet he boasted that without him a man was quite useless and could never hope to be a soldier! The next one, 'Index,' was always poking into everything—and he was always pointing. He claimed he guided the pen when something had to be written! The middle one was taller than the rest—he towered above them—and was always bragging about that! The next one wore a gold band round his waist—and you can imagine how conceited that made him! And the littlest one never did a stroke of work and seemed to think he should be admired for that! It was brag and boast, brag

99

and boast from morning till night! I got so tired of it, I decided to get out: I simply let myself fall into the sink and be washed away!"

"And here we both sit glittering!" said the bit of glass. At that moment some more water came swirling down the gutter, and swept the bit of glass out of sight.

"Well, he's moved on!" said the darning needle. "However, I prefer to stay here quietly. I'm so very delicate! Besides, it's much more dignified!" So she sat there proud and erect, deep in thought.

"I'm so very fine—so delicate," she said softly to herself. "I sometimes think I must have been born of a sunbeam. I notice the sun always manages to find me in the water. My mother can never seem to find me—I'm too fine for her! It's really very sad—if my eye hadn't been snapped off, I think I might start to cry! That wouldn't do, though—I'm too fine and delicate for that!"

One day some street urchins were poking about in the gutter. Sometimes they'd find an old nail, or a lost penny or two. It was a messy game, but they enjoyed it.

"Ouch!" cried one of them as he pricked himself on the darning needle. "Dirty old beast, you!"

"I am not a dirty old beast—I am a refined young lady," said the darning needle. But no one seemed to hear her. She'd lost her sealing wax, and had turned quite black— but then black is so becoming! "I'm slimmer and more delicate than ever!" she said to herself.

"Look!" shouted one of the boys. "Here comes an eggshell sailing down the gutter!"

He seized the darning needle and stuck her upright in the eggshell like a mast.

"These white walls form a perfect background for my slim black figure," murmured the darning needle. "How distinguished I must look! I only hope I shan't get seasick; I might break—I might break!"

But she didn't get seasick, and she didn't break.

"That shows what an advantage it is to have a steel stomach," she said to herself. "And then one should always remember that one is a little better than just ordinary people! I'm quite recovered now! The more delicate one is, the more one can endure."

"Cra-a-a-ak!" cried the eggshell, as a heavy wagon wheel rolled over it. "Oh! What a weight!" moaned the darning

needle. "I'm going to be seasick after all! I shall break! I shall break!" But although a heavy wagon wheel had rolled right over her, she didn't break. She just lay there full-length in the road. And—I think we've had enough of her! Let's leave her there!

IT'S
ABSOLUTELY TRUE!

"IT'S THE MOST frightful story!" said a hen to her companions. Now these particular hens lived in a part of town a long way from where the story was supposed to have taken place. "To think that a thing like that should happen in a hen house!" she continued. "I tell you—! I'd be scared to sleep alone at night. Thank goodness there are so many of us here—we can crowd close together on the perches." And then she told them the whole story. The other hens were so scared their feathers stood on end with terror, and the rooster's scarlet comb drooped and turned quite pale.

But perhaps we'd better start at the beginning. It all began in a hen house way over on the other side of town. It was evening. The sun went down, and the hens flew up—to their perches. One of them—a  little white hen with squatty legs who laid her egg regularly every day and was considered most proper and respectable—sat preening her feathers with her beak before she went to sleep, and one tiny little white feather fluttered to the ground. "There goes a feather!" she cried. "Well—they say a little thinning out improves the appearance. No doubt the more I preen myself the prettier I'll be!''

She only said this in fun, you know. She was a jolly little hen, in spite of being so respectable.

By now it was quite dark in the chicken house. Most of the hens were fast asleep, huddled together on the perches. But the little white hen's neighbor was still awake. She had heard—and yet not heard, if you know what I mean. Sometimes that's the wisest thing to do if you want to live in peace! All the same, she couldn't resist mentioning it to the hen on the other side of her. "Did you hear that remark?" she said. "We won't mention any names—but there's a certain hen here who wants to make herself attractive by plucking out her feathers. If I were the rooster, I'd treat her with contempt!"

Now, right above this hen house, in a big tree, lived the Owl family: Mother Owl, Father Owl, and all the little Owls. They had such sharp ears that they overheard every word the hen was saying. They rolled their eyes, and Mother Owl fanned herself with her wings. "Don't listen! Don't listen!" she cried. "Still, you couldn't very well have helped hearing it—I heard it with my own ears. What is the world coming to? One of those hens down there has so far forgotten all henly decency that she's actually plucking out all her feathers—and in the presence of the rooster too!"

"Sh! Prenez-garde aux enfants! The children! The children!" muttered Father

108

Owl. "It would never do for them to hear such things!"

"I must just tell my friend the Owl across the way," said Mother Owl. "She's such a worthy soul—she'd never forgive me if I kept this from her!" And off she flew.

"Hu-hu! Hu-hu uhuh!" she called to her neighbor—and they hooted together over the news.

They were sitting right above a dovecote,

and they called down to the doves below: "Hu-hu! Hu-hu uhuh! Have you heard? Have you heard? There's a hen who has plucked out all her feathers for love of the rooster! She's freezing to death—in fact, some say she's dead already! Hu-hu! Hu-hu uhuh!"

"Where? Where?" asked the doves.

"In that hen house across the way," answered Mother Owl. "I as good as saw it with my own eyes. I'm almost ashamed to talk about it, but it's absolutely true! Hu-hu! Hu-hu uhuh!"

"Trrrrue, trrrrue, trrrrrue!" cooed the doves, and they called out to the chickens in their own barnyard: "There's a hen—in fact, some say that there are two—who have plucked out all their feathers just to be different; just to attract the attention of the rooster! It's a dangerous game. There's the risk of catching cold and dying of a fever. And that's just what happened to them— for they are dead! Yes! Both of them are dead! Trrrrue, trrrrue, trrrrrue!"

"Cock-a-doodle-do! Wa-a-a-ake up!" crowed the rooster. He flapped his wings and flew up onto the fence. His eyes were still full of sleep, but he kept on crowing all the same: "Three hens have died of a broken heart—all for the love of a rooster! Cock-a-doodle-do! They had plucked out all their feathers and were frozen to death! It's such a nasty story, I don't care to hang on to it. So, pass it on—pass it on—pa-a-ass it on!"

"We will! We will!" squeaked the bats. And the hens clucked, "Paaas! Pass, pass, pass, pass it on! Paaas—pass, pass, pass, pass it on!" And the roosters crowed, "Cock-a-doodle-do! Pa-a-ass it on!" And the story traveled from one hen house to another all over the town, until at last it got back to the hen house where it had actually started. "There are five hens"—that's how the story went by now—"there are five hens who plucked out all their feathers to prove which one had grown thinnest for love of the rooster! Then they pecked at one another till they were covered in blood, and all five dropped down dead! A shame and a disgrace to their relatives, and a serious loss to their owner."

Now, the little white hen who had lost one tiny little feather naturally didn't recognize her own story; and because she was so very proper and respectable, she cried: "I despise such hens! Unfortunately there are plenty of that sort. I consider it my duty to spread this story far and wide. In fact, I shall do my best to get it into the newspaper. It will serve as a warning, and it's no more than those dreadful hens deserve—and their relatives as well!''

And the story did get into the newspaper —it was printed there in black and white.

So, you see—it's absolutely true! One tiny little white feather can actually turn into five dead hens!

THE STEADFAST
TIN SOLDIER

ONCE UPON A TIME there were twenty-five tin soldiers. They were brothers, for they had all been made out of the same old tin spoon. They shouldered arms, stood at attention "eyes front!" and wore the most splendid blue and scarlet uniforms.

114

The very first thing they heard, when the lid was lifted off their box, were the words "Tin soldiers!"

"Tin soldiers!" shouted the little boy as he clapped his hands for joy. It was his birthday, and the tin soldiers had been given to him for a birthday present. Right away, he took them all out of their box and lined them up on the table. They were all exactly alike—all but one. He was different, for he had only one leg. When they got around to making him, there wasn't quite enough tin left to finish him off properly. But he stood just as firmly on his one leg as the others did on their two—and of all these tin soldiers he's the one who became famous.

There were a lot of other toys scattered about on the table, and the most exciting

thing of all was a lovely cardboard castle. You could look through the tiny windows and see into all the different rooms. Just outside the castle, some little trees were grouped round a piece of mirror that looked just like a lake. It even had wax swans floating about on it—you could see them reflected in its surface. The effect was very pretty! But the prettiest thing of all was a dainty little lady who stood in the open doorway of the castle. She was made out of cardboard too, but her little skirt was made of real gauze, and over her shoulder was draped a narrow blue ribbon held in place by a large spangle—it was almost as large as the whole of her face, and it sparkled just like a diamond.

The little lady was a dancer; so, of course, she was standing on one toe, with her arms outstretched. Her other leg was raised so high that the tin soldier couldn't even see it, so he took it for granted that she too had only one leg. "Just like me," he thought.

"What a wife she'd make me!" he said to himself. "Only, I suppose, she's much too grand—after all, she lives in a castle, while all I have is a box! And it doesn't even belong to me—there are twenty-five of us to share it. I'd never dare ask her to live there! All the same, I'd like to get to know her." He flung himself down full length, and hid behind a snuffbox that was standing on the table. From there he was able to watch the pretty little lady, who kept standing on one leg without ever losing her balance.

Later in the evening the other soldiers were put back in their box. The people who lived in the house all went to bed— and then the toys began to play. They played at "visiting," they played at "war," they played at "giving parties." Inside their box the tin soldiers were all rattling about —they would have liked to join the fun, but they couldn't get the lid off. The nut-crackers turned somersaults, and the slate pencil danced a jig all over the slate. There was such a lot of noise that the canary woke up with a start and began chattering away— in verse, if you please! But the tin soldier  and the little dancer remained quite still: she stood erect on the tip of her toe, with both arms outstretched; and he on his one leg was steadfast too, and never took his eyes off her.

Then the clock struck twelve, and, sud-denly, the lid of the snuffbox flew open with a bang. It was a trick snuffbox—there was no snuff in it at all, only a little black imp who popped out now and then just to scare people.

"Tin soldier!" shouted the imp. "Keep your eyes to yourself!"

The tin soldier pretended not to hear.

119

"You just wait till tomorrow!" said the imp.

Well, when tomorrow came, the children got up, and the tin soldier was moved over to the window sill. Now it might have been the fault of the imp, or it might have been a sudden gust of wind, but the window suddenly blew open and the tin soldier fell headfirst from the third floor right down to the street below. It was a terrible fall! When he came to, he found himself with his leg in the air and the point of his bayonet wedged into the pavement.

The maid and the little boy rushed down into the street to look for him; but though they came so close to him they nearly stepped on him, they couldn't find him. If only he had called out, "Look! Here I am!" they would certainly have found him. But

he didn't think it right to raise his voice while he was in uniform.

Then it began to rain. The rain came down faster and faster and turned into a regular deluge. When at last it stopped, two street urchins came along.

"Hey! Look!" one said to the other. "There's a tin soldier. Let's send him for a sail!"

So they made a little boat out of an old newspaper, put the tin soldier in it, and off he sailed down the gutter. The two boys ran along beside him clapping their hands. It had rained so hard that there were great waves in the gutter, and there was a powerful current. The paper boat rocked up and down, and twirled round and round till the poor tin soldier felt quite sick and dizzy. But he remained steadfast, never changed his expression, gazed straight before him, and kept on shouldering arms.

All of a sudden the boat swept under a plank that had been placed lengthwise across the gutter. It was terribly dark under there—like being in his box with the lid on, the tin soldier thought.

"I wonder where I'm off to now?" he said to himself. "It's all the fault of that horrid black imp! If only the pretty little lady were here beside me, it could be twice as dark for all I'd care!"

Just then out popped a huge water rat who lived under the plank.

"Where's your permit?" shouted the rat. "Come on! Show your permit!"

But the tin soldier made no answer. He clutched his rifle more firmly than ever. The boat rushed on and the rat after it. He ground his teeth ferociously and screamed out to all the sticks and straws: "Stop him! Stop him! He hasn't paid his toll and he hasn't shown his permit!"

The current was getting swifter and swifter. The tin soldier could see daylight now at the end of the tunnel, but he also heard a dreadful roaring noise—it was enough to scare the bravest of men. Just think! At the end of the plank, the water from the gutter gushed out into a great canal. The tin soldier was in grave danger. If you can imagine being swept over a huge waterfall in a little canoe, you'll know just how he felt!

But by now he was so near the brink that it was too late to stop. The boat shot out into the canal, the poor tin soldier did his best to stand stiffly at attention. He wasn't going to give anyone the chance to say he'd so much as blinked an eye. The boat whirled round several times and was filled to the brim with water. It was bound to sink. The tin soldier was up to his neck in water and the boat sank deeper and deeper. The paper began to fall apart; then the water closed over the soldier's head. He thought of the lovely little dancer whom he would never see again, and an old song kept ringing in his ears:

Brave soldier, here is danger;
Brave soldier, here is death!

Then the paper gave way beneath his feet and down he went. But at that very moment a big fish came along, opened its mouth, and swallowed him in a gulp.

My goodness, how dark it was inside that fish! Even darker than in the tunnel; and there was scarcely room to breathe! Still, the tin soldier remained steadfast. He kept on shouldering arms, even though he was lying on his side. The fish leaped about and made the most terrifying contortions. Then, suddenly, it grew quite still. Something like a streak of lightning seemed to flash through it—and then it was broad daylight. A voice called out, "The tin soldier!" The fish had been caught, had been taken to market and sold, and was now in the kitchen, where the cook had just cut it open with her large kitchen knife.

She seized the tin soldier round the middle and carried him into the living room to show him off. There he was much admired. After all, very few men have traveled about inside a fish! But he wasn't a bit conceited. They stood him up on the table, and then he saw—really life is quite remarkable at times!—he saw that he was back in the very same room he'd been in before. There were the very same children, and the very

125

same toys spread out on the table. There was the lovely castle, and there stood the pretty little dancer in the doorway. She was still balanced on one leg, her other leg held high in the air, and her little arms outstretched. She too had remained steadfast. The tin soldier was deeply moved—he almost shed tin tears. But, of course, he couldn't cry because he was in uniform. He gazed at her, and she gazed back at him, but neither of them said a word.

Suddenly—for no apparent reason—one of the little boys picked up the tin soldier and threw him into the stove. The horrid black imp in the snuffbox must have put it into his head.

The tin soldier stood in the bright glare and felt the most terrible heat. Was it the heat of the coals? Or the heat of love? He couldn't be quite sure. The bright colors of his uniform were all streaked and faded, but whether this was the result of his journey, or the result of sorrow, no one could tell. He gazed at the pretty little lady, and she gazed back at him. He felt himself melting away, but he still stood there steadfast and kept on shouldering arms.

A door was suddenly opened, and there was a gust of wind. It snatched up the little dancer, and she flew like a sylph into the stove straight to the tin soldier, blazed up into a flame, and disappeared. Then the tin soldier melted down into a little lump, and the next day when the maid emptied out the ashes, she found him in the shape of a tiny tin heart. But all that was left of the dancer was the spangle—and that was burned as black as coal.